HOW THE ANIMALS GOT THEIR COLOURS

To Geraldine, Joe, Naomi, Eddie, Laura and Isaac. MR

To my family. With special thanks to Miriam. JC

First published in 1991 by Studio Editions Ltd, Princess House,
50 Eastcastle Street, London WIN 7AP, England

ISBN 1 85170 730 1

Printed and bound in Hong Kong

Designed by Bridget Long, The Design Works, Reading, England

Sources

COYOTE 'Zuñi Tales' Edward Handy, reprinted by permission of the
American Folklore Society from the *Journal of American Folklore*
31:121, 1918, not for further reproduction; FLYING FISH *Papuan Fairy Tales*
Annie Kerr (Macmillan, London, 1910); FROG *The Golden Age of Myth
and Fable* Thomas Bulfinch (Bracken Books, London, 1985); TIGER *Songs
and Stories of the Chu'an Miao* David Crockett Graham (Smithsonian
Institution, Washington DC, 1954); BROLGA Adapted from *The Dawn of
Time – Australian Aboriginal Myths* Ainslie Roberts and Charles
P Mountford (Art Australia, Australia, 1989); LEOPARD 'Folk Tales From
Liberia' Richard Bundy, reprinted by permission of the American Folklore
Society from the *Journal of American Folklore* 125:406, 1919, not for
further reproduction; PEACOCK *Folk Tales of the Khāsis* Mrs Rafy
(Macmillan, London, 1920); CRANE *The King of the Snakes*
Rosetta Baskerville (Sheldon Press, Uganda, 1922); HOW THE ANIMALS GOT
THEIR COLOURS Adapted, with permission, from Johannes Wilbert and
Karin Simoneau, eds, *Folk Literature of the Ayoreo Indians* (Los Angeles:
UCLA Latin American Center Publications, University of California,
1989), Narrative 54, 'Sun Paints Animals', pp 102-103.

HOW THE ANIMALS GOT THEIR COLOURS

Michael Rosen

illustrated by John Clementson

STUDIO EDITIONS

LONDON

Storyteller's note

All over the world, people saw the animals and wondered
how they came to be just as they were. The people answered
their questions by making up stories. The tales that they told
took place long, long ago, sometimes before the first humans
were born. The people told the stories to their children, who
told them to their children in turn. The people that spoke
them believed in them. They lived by their truths. They
made up dances and ceremonies to celebrate them.

As the words pass down from storyteller to storyteller we
can listen to them and write them down, as we have done
here. Enjoy them now, the stories of people all over the world.

Contents

Coyote

Coyote is a wild dog. He thinks he's so cunning, so clever. Mr Wiseguy. When he's hungry he goes out and he catches himself just whatever creature he wants. His favourite is goose.

One day he comes to a little river and there's a whole crowd of them swimming around in there. Coyote lies down with his head on his paws to watch for a while. One by one, they come to the river's edge and climb up onto the bank. Then one old goose says, "Ready? Then jump!" And they all jump into the water, swim around for a bit and then start all over again.

"Hey! What are you guys doing?" says Coyote.

"Oh, what we're doing," they say, "is we come up here on the riverbank, take our eyes out and throw them in the water. Then we jump in after them and those eyes just jump right back into our heads."

Coyote thinks about this. It sounds like fun.

"Say you guys, what do you say to me joining in? Can I play?"

"Sure," say the geese. "Come on in."

Coyote takes out his eyes. Coyote throws his eyes in the water. Coyote jumps in the water and those eyes jump right back into his head.

"Well, what do you know!" shouts Coyote. "This is just great. Woweee!"

So Coyote does it again. And again and again and again.

"Wowee! This is just about the best bit of fun I've had in years," he says.

But the geese start getting tired of him. There's no need to get quite so excited about it, they think. All we're doing is taking our eyes out, throwing them in the river and jumping in after them. No big deal.

"Hey, what do you say to this?" says one goose, real quiet to his friend. "He throws his eyes in and we get in there and steal them."

"Nice," says his friend. "I like it."

Coyote throws in his eyes. "Wowee! There they go again," he shouts.

And just as quick as you like, the geese whip those eyes out of the water and they're off, away.

Coyote jumps in. No eyes. His eyes aren't there. They don't jump back into his head.

"Ayee, geese! You've tricked me. You don't want me to see, right? I get it. Steal his eyes and old Coyote won't know where he is, right? Well, listen here, geese. I'm coming after you and I'm going to eat you up, from top to toe. Every little feather on your heads."

"Come and get us then, Coyote. Come and get us," shout the geese.

Up jumps Coyote. He's out of the river and he's running down the riverbank after them. But the river turns and next thing, splash! He's back in the river. He can't see a thing.

"I'll catch them," says Coyote, and he reaches down and finds a couple of pebbles. He puts them in his eyeholes.

"I can see you now," he shouts. "Least, I will in just a moment," he mutters to himself as he fiddles with the pebbles trying to make them work like eyes. But nothing. They don't work. And they drop out. On he runs. Round and round. Seeing nothing, finding nothing, until he bumps right into a cactus.

"Ayee," shouts Coyote, "cactus! Aha … cactus. I know cactus, with the big yellow berries. Find one, Coyote. Find one."

So Coyote feels over the cactus with his paw. The prickles hurt him.

"Ayee, it must be here, there must be one." And, sure enough, Coyote finds a big yellow cactus berry and he puts it in his eyehole.

"Hey, I can see. Now, Coyote, that was smart. Now just find yourself another one to match."

Off goes Coyote again, the one cactus-berry-eye in his head, looking for more cactus berries. And he finds one. Puts it in. Two yellow eyes.

"Now for the geese," he says.

But the geese are gone. Not one in sight. And off goes Coyote, hunting those geese. And he's still out there hunting them today. Now you know why. And something else. Now you know how he got those angry yellow eyes.

Flying Fish

In the old days before the old days there was only dry land. No one knew that the sea was bottled up in a tree.

In the old days before the old days there was an old man and his wife. She was sick so he hunted for food for her.

One day he whistled for his dog but his dog didn't come. He found it beneath the sea-tree, eating strange shining pieces.

The old man tasted them and found them to be sweet and soft in his mouth. He took them to his wife who ate them and fell asleep.

When she awoke she was better and longed for more of the strange shining pieces. The old man led many others to the sea-tree.

As they watched, a great wave flowed out of the sea-tree and they saw that the shining pieces were flying fish.

Some people waited for more. Others couldn't wait and wanted to chop the tree down, so they fetched axes.

Down came the tree and the sea with all its fish flowed out. But the flying fish knew man and hid in the mud.

Women went out and found them, fished for them. In the gardens the weeds grew and smothered the roots and berries the people used to eat.

The women fished on and on. From the sound of the first bird of the morning till the sun set in the sea, they fished for flying fish.

The old man saw that soon there would be no fish left and he went among the fish, saying, "Go, go and live far out at sea and we will seek you out only when the time is right."

But the flying fish stayed, sinking deeper into the mud to keep from the women's sight.

So the old man took up pieces of broken coral and hurled them at the flying fish, saying, "Go now if you want to live. Go now so that we may always have flying fish to hunt."

When the pieces of broken coral hit the flying fish, they took off and fled from the old man, taking themselves far out to sea.

Look now at the flying fish and you will see pink marks on their heads, made by the coral the old man threw when he first sent them far out to sea.

Frog

Back in the days when people knew that gods and goddesses could come down to earth, Latona, daughter of the gods, was hurrying through some woods, carrying her two baby children.

She was looking for somewhere to rest; somewhere she could find fresh water to drink, for she and her children had mouths as dry as dust. Her eyes fell on some country people, hard at work gathering reeds to make baskets. Close by them was a pool of lovely clear water.

Latona ran to the waterside, knelt down, and just as she was about to feel the cool, wet taste on her tongue, the country people stopped her.

"No, madam! Drinking from this water is not allowed."

Latona was furious.

"Not allowed? Water is like the air and the sunshine – it is free for all of us to use, and I have come to take my share. And listen – I won't wash in it, I won't bathe my tired legs in it, I won't stir up the mud. All I want is to quench my thirst. My mouth is so dry, I can hardly speak. One taste of this water would be heaven. Can't you see my little children stretching out their arms – begging for me?"

But the country people wouldn't move.

"The water is not for you. If we let any old tramp like you come here and drink, there'd be none left for us. Now clear off!"

"I tell you what," said one, "let's stop her and her brats drinking any of it," and they rushed into the pool and stirred up the mud on the bottom until the water was cloudy and green.

Latona could have wept. But instead of pleading with the people, she lifted her hands to heaven and called out, "May these people never leave the pool! May they pass the rest of their living days in it."

And so it was. They now live in the pool – sometimes underwater, sometimes lifting their heads above the surface, sometimes swimming along, sometimes sitting on the bank and sometimes leaping back in. They still shout and complain, though they have all the water to themselves. Their voices are harsh and their throats bloated. Their mouths are stretched wide from all the complaining they do, and their necks have shrivelled so that their heads are now joined to their bodies. Their bellies are white but their backs are the colour of the mud they stirred up to stop Latona drinking – green.

What are they?

Tiger

A meeting is taking place on Great Mountain.

Tiger says Tiger's the best, the strongest, the fastest on earth. Thunder says Thunder's the best, the loudest, the fiercest on earth. Echo says Echo's the best, the toughest, the cleverest on earth. Dragon says Dragon's the best, the mightiest, the hottest on earth.

"Yes, yes, yes," says Tiger, "I know all about you, but the thing that makes me the best is that I'm not afraid of anything."

Tiger, Thunder, Echo and Dragon cannot decide who is the greatest.

"Let us have a contest," says Tiger, "and in this contest we will see which of us is the most terrifying. Whoever can make the other three say, 'Stop, no more' is the winner."

They agree, and Tiger laughs.

"Now I'll show them."

Tiger paws the ground, opens its jaws, shows every tooth in its head and roars. Thunder vanishes into thin air and sits among the clouds. Echo rolls down Great Mountain, across Blue River, up Little Mountain and is gone. Dragon coils and twists its long body and tail and squirms its way up into the sky, out of reach of Tiger's claws.

No one says, 'Stop, no more'. Tiger is left pawing the ground and roaring to itself till there is no roar left. Thunder, Echo and Dragon come back.

"Tiger loses," they say.

"I know, I know, I know," says Tiger.

Now Thunder comes forward, looks around at the clouds and then flies off to the deepest, darkest one in sight. From that cloud comes the most horrendous drumming, deafening rolls.

Tiger can't bear it and shouts, "Stop, no more!"

But Echo listens to the Thunder rolls, waits for them at the top of Little Mountain and rolls them back at Thunder.

And Dragon just coils and twists its long body and tail and squirms its way up into the sky, up above Thunder's clouds where it is all quiet.

Thunder, Echo and Dragon come back.

"Thunder loses," they say.

"I'm better than Tiger," says Thunder.

"I know, I know, I know," says Tiger.

Now Echo comes forward and waits.

"Well, aren't you going to start?" says Tiger.

"Going to start?" says Echo.

"Well, don't hang about," says Tiger.

"Don't hang about," says Echo.

"It's not me that's hanging about, you fool," says Tiger.

"You fool," says Echo.

"Who are you calling a fool?" asks Tiger.

"Who are you calling a fool?" asks Echo.

"You," says Tiger.

"You," says Echo.

"Just get on with it," roars Tiger.

"Get on with it," roars Echo.

"It's not my turn," says Tiger.

"It's not my turn," says Echo.

"It is," says Tiger.

"It is," says Echo.

"You're driving me mad," shouts Tiger.

"You're driving me mad," shouts Echo.

"Stop, stop, no more," says Tiger.

"Stop, stop, no more," says Echo.

"I agree," says Thunder.

"I agree," says Echo.

"Stop, no more," says Thunder.

Echo looks round for Dragon but Dragon has coiled and twisted up its long body and tail and squirmed away up into the sky where not even an Echo can reach. Some time later, Dragon comes back.

"Echo loses," they say.

"Echo was better than Thunder," says Dragon.

"Better than Thunder," says Echo.

"That's true," says Thunder.

"Echo was better than Tiger," says Dragon.

"Better than Tiger," says Echo.

"I know, I know, I know," says Tiger.

Now it is Dragon's turn. Dragon coils and twists its long body and tail and pours fire out of its mouth. Thunder flies to its cloud, but Dragon follows and breathes fire on the cloud and dries it up till there is nowhere for Thunder to sit.

"Stop, no more," shouts Thunder.

Dragon chases Echo down Great Mountain, across Blue River, up Little Mountain till they meet going down the other side.

"Do you want to give up?" asks Dragon.

"Give up," says Echo.

"Stop, no more?" asks Dragon.

"Stop, no more," says Echo.

"And now for Tiger," said Dragon. But Tiger is hiding in the forest on the side of Great Mountain. So Dragon coils and twists up its long body and tail and lets fly a huge jet of flame and sets that forest on fire. But Tiger is ready for it and runs from the fire that races through the trees. And Tiger would have escaped but for the wind in the treetops that flew even faster. Just as Tiger is leaving the forest behind, the fire crackles overhead. The flaming branches of a tree fall on Tiger, just as it thinks it is free.

"Stop, no more," shouts Tiger.

"I've won," says Dragon.

"That's true," says Thunder.

"That's true," says Echo.

"Never mind that," says Tiger, "look at my coat, the branches have burnt my fur."

"Yes," says Dragon, "you're all stripy."

"I know, I know, I know," says Tiger.

22

Brolga

No one could dance like Brolga
No one could dance like Brolga

Everyone came to see her dancing. The women beat the ground to the rhythm of her steps. The men danced along with her and one by one stepped forward hoping to marry her.

One was Nonega. He was evil. He could make magic. How he wanted to marry her! But the old men of the tribe said no. They didn't want Brolga to marry anyone so evil.

"If I can't have Brolga," said Nonega, "then no one else will."

No one could dance like Brolga
No one could dance like Brolga

One day Brolga danced on her own out on the plain. But nearer and nearer, a whirlwind came rushing towards her, and in the middle of the whirlwind was Nonega. As it roared across the plain it sucked up dry dust into itself. The air whirled faster and faster over Brolga's face until the whirlwind was upon her. It wrapped itself around her until she disappeared in a cloud of dust.

For a while the whirlwind twisted there, then passed on. But now there was no sign of Brolga. In her place stood a tall bird, as grey as the whirlwind's dust. It swayed and waved its wings just as Brolga had danced.

When the people saw the bird, they called out, "Brolga! Brolga!"

The bird seemed to hear them and danced and danced while the women beat the ground to the rhythm of its steps.

And a tall bird can still be seen out on the plains of northern Australia, swaying and waving its wings, with feathers as grey as a whirlwind's dust.

No one could dance like Brolga
No one could dance like Brolga

Leopard

See Leopard. He can leap so quick he's out of sight before you've blinked. Watch him. See Nyomo. His eyes are so good, he can stand at the bottom of a tree and see a fly on the topmost leaf. Watch him. You've heard of Lion? Wait for him. He comes later.

One day Leopard says to Nyomo, "Let's go, you and me, and find wild honey." They walk, Leopard's paws pad on the ground, foop, foop, foop. Nyomo's feet glide beside Leopard, shoo, shoo, shoo.

"Look there!" says Leopard. "A bees' nest. I am the first to see the nest." They take a look inside.

"No honey," says Nyomo, "walk on." They walk. Foop, foop, foop, go Leopard's paws. Shoo, shoo, shoo, go Nyomo's feet.

"Look there!" says Nyomo. "A bees' nest. I am the first to see a nest full of honey!" They take a look inside.

"Honey!" says Nyomo. "Let's eat."

And they eat honey till their bellies are full and their eyes go wild.

"Leopard," says Nyomo, "give yourself a name. What name do you want to call yourself?"

"Strong-man," says Leopard. "And you?"

"I'm Iron-man," says Nyomo. "And Iron-man is a better name than Strong-man." Leopard growls at that. Leopard snarls, Leopard rages. He seizes Nyomo, ties a rope around his middle and drags him along. They meet Barking-deer.

"Say, Leopard, don't you know better than to go dragging Lion's brother along like that?"

"I know what I know," says Leopard. "You just mind your own business, Barking-deer."

"Say, Nyomo," says Barking-deer, "will *you* tell me what's going on here?"

"I said Iron-man was a better name than Strong-man, and Iron-man is the name I'm going to have."

Barking-deer laughs. He laughs and laughs till it hurts.

"You? Nyomo? Iron-man? Little Nyomo who can't lift a log, can't bite a bone and couldn't even fight a fly – you dare to call yourself Iron-man in front of Leopard? You deserve everything you get."

Leopard is thinking: Nyomo is Lion's brother! So, I'll take him to Lion and he'll soon tell Nyomo who's who around here. Leopard drags Nyomo to Lion. And when Lion sees his brother tied up he is furious. He is enraged. Lion tells Leopard right there what to do.

"Set Nyomo free," says Lion. Leopard sets Nyomo free.

"Fetch water," says Lion. Leopard fetches water.

"Fill the bath," says Lion. Leopard fills the bath.

"Nyomo, my brother, bath yourself in the clear, cool water." Nyomo climbs into the bath.

"Leopard, get under the bath and stay there." Leopard gets under the bath. Nyomo's hot, dry, dusty skin softens and shines in the bath but the dirty water, full of the dust, dribbles over Leopard. Leopard growls, "rrrr, rrrr, rrrr."

Now Nyomo rests. Lion and his wife bring food and sit with Nyomo, eating. They eat and eat till all that's left is bits of bones, peel and husks.

"Nyomo, dear brother," says Lion, pointing to the scraps, "why not take these delicious little tit-bits to Leopard?"

Nyomo takes the bits of bones, peel and husks to Leopard and this drives Leopard into a roaring rage.

"Lion," roars Leopard, "I'll tear you into so many pieces it'll take ten years to count the bits." Lion doesn't move.

"Lion, I'll throw you so high you won't come down till next year." Lion doesn't move.

"Lion, I'll squash you so flat, you'll blow away on the wind like a leaf." Lion moves. Lion rises. Lion pounces on Leopard. Leopard fights back. Biting, clawing, raging. Every bit Leopard bites out of Lion, he swallows. Every bit Lion bites out of Leopard, he lays on the ground.

See who's coming: Old Mother. She comes near and sees Lion and Leopard locked together, fighting in the hot dust. She sees Lion tearing at Leopard.

"Run Leopard!" she cries. "Run Leopard, before Lion kills you."

So Leopard runs. He runs and runs till he finds a pool of cool mud. With his paws he picks up pats of mud and, fap, fap, fap, he pats it into the holes Lion made. Fap, fap, fap, he closes them over till there are no holes left. Then, Leopard lies down to get better.

Everything's fine for Leopard now but his skin stays spotty forever.

Peacock

In the beginning, Peacock was just a dull, grey bird and yet he went about boasting and bragging.

"I am the most magnificent creature on earth. You are all so fortunate in having the chance to cast your eyes upon me," he would say.

The other birds could not bear this talk but they gathered round Peacock, saying, "Peacock, you're fantastic. You're really beautiful, you know. So lovely to look at."

And Peacock would puff out his chest and strut about even more while the other birds flew off fit to burst with laughter.

One day the birds made up a story.

"Peacock," they said, "out of all the birds in the jungle, we've chosen you to carry our best wishes to the lovely lady Ka Sngi who lives up, up, up in the Blue Kingdom of the Sky."

Peacock was delighted. "And what a good choice I am. Yes, it is I, Peacock, who has been selected to pay respects to Ka Sngi, she who pours out her bright light on us here on earth. I will win this great lady as my wife and live with her in the Blue Kingdom of the Sky."

The birds laughed among themselves. "Him! He's so fat he can hardly fly as high as a hedge!"

But Peacock said goodbye to them all and took off. Up, up, up he flew until he was out of sight. On he travelled until he landed at the dazzling palace of Ka Sngi, the lovely lady of the Blue Kingdom of the Sky.

Peacock bowed low. "I, Peacock, bring best wishes from all the birds on earth."

Happy Ka Sngi! All her life she had lived alone and now, at long last, someone had come to see her.

"Oh come in, sir, you are more than welcome. Come live with me and I will never be alone again."

She smiled and her light shone out over all the world.

Peacock became her husband, but as every day passed he became more selfish, more boastful, more demanding.

He spoke to Ka Sngi, saying, "Why should you, my wife, show so much care for the world, shining your light on those dull, ordinary creatures down there. You should shine all your light on me, Peacock."

Ka Sngi did what Peacock asked, and no light reached the earth. The whole world became dark and cold. The birds in the jungle stopped singing and their feathers drooped.

Finally, they could stand it no longer and went to see a wise old woman.

She spoke to them, saying, "All the people are in despair. Now that the earth is cold and dark, our crops won't grow. What little we have, you birds eat. All that I have left are a few mustard seeds. But listen! Promise me two things: stop eating my seeds, and drive off the animals that eat my crops. If you do this, I will bring Peacock back to earth so that we may all enjoy the light and warmth of Ka Sngi."

The birds agreed and the wise old woman set to work. She planted her mustard seeds in the ground in the shape of a woman. The seeds sprouted, and when the flowers came out, it looked as if a beautiful golden lady lay on the ground.

Up in the Blue Kingdom of the Sky, Peacock looked down and saw the mustard flowers.

He turned to Ka Sngi, saying, "Down on earth, I observe that there is a beautiful golden lady. I feel attracted to her, and I am sure that if she were to see me, she would immediately fall madly in love with me. I can tarry here with you no longer."

Poor Ka Sngi! All her life she had lived alone and now she was losing the only companion she had ever had.

"I beg you, stay! Stay!"

And as she pleaded with Peacock, she wept great tears. The drops fell on his dull, grey tail. The moment they touched his tail feathers they became brilliantly coloured spots.

Ka Sngi called after Peacock, saying, "These spots are a sign. Now you will never be able to forget me, Ka Sngi, the most lovely and caring of women."

Peacock flew back to earth to meet the beautiful golden lady on the ground.

"Ah, you birds, I am back. Would you be so kind as to convey me at great speed to see the golden beauty I observed from my palace on high?"

"Oh yes, your majesty, we'd love to take you to see her," they said, and took him to see the mustard flowers.

When Peacock saw that his golden lady was nothing but a few flowers he was struck dumb. He felt so foolish.

"Ah, but no matter," he said to himself, "there is always my lovely Ka Sngi in the sky."

And so he started to flap his wings to fly back up to her. But now, no matter how hard he tried and tried, he could fly no higher than a nearby tree.

And ever since this time, every morning, Peacock stretches his neck and flaps his wings to greet the coming of the light of Ka Sngi from her Blue Kingdom of the Sky. And the only happiness he can find here on earth is to spread his lovely feathers, marked with Ka Sngi's tears, so that her light can shine on them.

Crane

Princess Namirembe of Uganda sits in her father's great canoe.
Listen to the men who paddle:

> *We are taking our Princess to the Island of Sesse*
> *Where the sands are smooth and bright,*
> *The forests deep and dark*
> *And the valleys cool and green.*
>
> *See our paddles dive into the water,*
> *See our paddles fly out of the water,*
> *See our paddles shoot through the air.*

Princess Namirembe of Uganda sits in her father's great canoe,
longing to travel further than the Island of Sesse. Listen to her
father, the King:

> *Wait, my daughter.*
> *Wait, watch and learn before you travel*
> *To places far and wide where the ways are strange.*

Princess Namirembe of Uganda picks fruit in her father's garden.
Listen to the crane:

> *Oh Princess, come,*
> *Come to Kavirondo,*
> *Far away over the great Lake*
> *To the wild country where the ways are strange.*
>
> *Come, sit on my back,*
> *Hold on to my feathers, my wings will steady you*
> *And close your eyes, for if you fall into the great Lake*
> *You will drown.*

Princess Namirembe of Uganda sits in Kavirondo while the crane flies off to visit his brother. Listen to the Princess:

> *I see great dark hills*
> *And a plain stretching further than my eye can see.*
> *Here I see warriors with helmets of cowrie shells,*
> *Ostrich feathers and beads painted white, yellow and red.*
> *White, yellow and red beads on the women*
> *From a village that hides behind a fence of high, hard wood.*
>
> *Here there are no green hills*
> *As there are in my Uganda.*
> *Here there are no green banana gardens*
> *No fruit trees, no grass, as there are in my Uganda.*

Princess Namirembe of Uganda sits on the crane's back. Listen to the crane:

> *We are high in the sky,*
> *Above islands so small no one lives there*
> *But for the diver birds making their nests among the rocks.*
> *Nothing else but sky, water and sun.*

Princess Namirembe of Uganda travels back to Uganda with the crane. Listen to the Princess:

> *Oh father, my beautiful Uganda with its lovely islands*
> *And ripe crops glowing pink in the setting sun.*
> *Let me tell you, oh father,*
> *Where the crane took me. The ways were strange*
> *And the land was flat and dry,*
> *Not like here in Uganda.*
> *Uganda, I won't ever leave again.*

Princess Namirembe of Uganda sits with her father and the crane. Listen to her father:

> *You, oh crane, I must thank*
> *For showing my daughter other places*
> *That make her happy to be here.*
> *I have a gift for you,*
> *A golden crest, dark at its root.*
> *Take it and wear it wherever you go.*

Listen to the storyteller tell you:

> *Look now at the crane and see his golden crest, dark at the root.*
> *Look now at the crane and see his golden crest, dark at the root.*

How the animals got their colours

Mighty Sun,
You who made woman,
You who made man,
You who made all the animals.

We remember how you painted Jaguar –
Dipping your hands into coal
You painted the spots on his coat;
But Jaguar, in a hurry as always,
Dashed away to show off his coat in the forest
And so the spots became blurred.

We remember how you painted Puma –
Seeing Jaguar, Puma came to you and said,
"Paint me too, so I might be as handsome as Jaguar."
You took two red stones, ground them together
And with the dust, you painted Puma.
"More colours," said Puma. "More colours."
But you told him that this was to be his colour for evermore.

We remember how you painted Snake –
Seeing Jaguar, Snake came to you and said,
"Paint me too, so I might be as handsome as Jaguar,
But paint me brighter, paint me bolder."
You took a yellow stone, ground it to powder
And with the powder, you rubbed Snake's skin.
Snake stretched herself, admired her shining coils.

We remember how you painted Rat Snake –
Seeing Jaguar, Rat Snake came to you and said,
"Paint me too, so I might be as handsome as Jaguar."
But you saw that you had no colours left
And so you dipped your hands into the coal
And painted Rat Snake black all over.
Rat Snake smiled at the sight of her skin.

Mighty Sun,
You who made woman,
You who made man,
You who made all the animals –
This is how you painted the animals.

About these stories

Coyote

UNITED STATES OF AMERICA

The people who tell this story are Zuñi Pueblo Native Americans from west and central New Mexico. In many Native American tales, animals arrive in the world before humans. For the Zuñi, Coyote is the most important animal of that time. Funny stories are told about him: sometimes he plays tricks, sometimes he is tricked and very often he is bad at hunting.

In the pueblos, life is centred round the family, or clan, and uncles and grandfathers help to bring up the children. Zuñi 'grandfathers' tell stories to children in winter, at home or when out visiting. When the story is finished, everyone makes a wish that their crops of corn, melon, onions and tomatoes will grow well that year.

The Coyote is a wild dog which lives on the western plains of North America. It is about 1.4 to 1.5 metres long, can run very swiftly and feeds on rodents, rabbits, deer, insects and fruit.

Flying Fish

PAPUA, NEW GUINEA

This story was told on the northeast coast of Papua, a province of the Pacific island of New Guinea. The folktales of this island are known as 'Vivarantua'. They are traditionally told to children by old women called 'dragoras', and by young married couples. A little magic verse is recited before the telling; each story has a tune of its own. Trees and plants, like the sea-tree, have a special place in explaining how the world was made.

Flying fish are found in the surface waters of all tropical seas and the Atlantic. By pushing themselves out of the water with their tails, they glide for several metres above water. They can be up to 30 centimetres long and feed on smaller fish.

Frog

ITALY

This story is told by the Roman poet Ovid in his famous book, *Metamorphoses*, about things changing shape. He retells a tale first told in Ancient Greece. Latona (Leto in Greek) was a daughter of the giant Titans. Loved by Zeus, greatest of the Greek gods, she was forced to flee by his jealous wife Hera. Afraid of Hera's anger, no one would receive Latona. Zeus anchored the magical, floating island of Delos so that she had a place in which to give birth to twins. The twins grew up to be Apollo, god of the sun and Artemis, goddess of the moon. The peasants in the story are from Lycia, a small country colonised by the Greeks in what is now southern Turkey.

The Greeks and Romans learnt to recite myths by heart. Professional singers would sing of the deeds of gods and heroes and great public occasions were linked to their stories. The tales were also told in beautiful writing and art.

The Common Frog is a smooth-skinned amphibian, found world-wide, but not native to Australia and New Zealand. It lives mostly on land, going to water to breed.

Tiger

CHINA

The Chu'an Miao, who tell this tale, live in the far northern mountain region of China. They are a very old people, mentioned in the writings of the Ancient Greeks. About 150,000 Chu'an Miao live in the Szechuan province of China today. They love singing and storytelling at marriages, funerals and the eating of new grain. Buffalo, herons and hens take part in a procession as the story is told, and the teller covers himself in ashes. The Tiger is the sign of Asia. It appears in many Asian myths, often cunning and greedy. The Dragon appears in myths all over the world, usually as an enemy, powerful and cruel. In China, the Dragon is said to hoard water and cause drought, especially in stories where it seeks refuge in the clouds.

The Tiger is a large, striped member of the big cat family, reaching over 3 metres in length. It lives in many parts of Asia in rainforest, grassland and mountains. It hunts by night and feeds on a variety of smaller animals.

Brolga

AUSTRALIA

For the Aborigines of northern Australia, stories of how
the world began are still a part of life today. At a festival
called a 'Corroboree', elders covered with colourful
patterns sing stories and make red, yellow, black and
white paintings on the rocks. The songs and paintings
speak of the 'Dreamtime', a time outside everyday time
when things became as they are now. They speak of the
making of mountains, rocks and hills, fish, birds and animals.
The stories teach us to care for the natural world around us.
If we harm the Brolga bird today we offend her ancestor who
still dances on the plains.

The Brolga bird lives on the farmlands and wetlands of northern
Australia. It can be 1.4 metres tall, and eats fish and insects.

Leopard

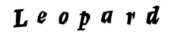

LIBERIA

This story was told to Richard Bundy in Liberia, where he worked
for the United States government in 1919. Liberia is a land of swamps,
sandy beaches, mountains and tropical rainforest and the people in each
region tell very different stories. Leopard's story comes from the Loma
people of the central mountains, and like many Loma tales shows tribal
law and custom at work. The man, Nyomo, is weak but must be treated with
respect as he is the 'brother' of Lion, the most powerful animal of all. Lion
treats Nyomo as an honoured guest.

The Leopard is a spotted big cat, found in the rainforest, grasslands, desert and
mountains of Africa and southern Asia. It can be up to 1.2 metres
long, is graceful, agile and a keen hunter, feeding on birds,
monkeys, baboons and antelope.

Peacock

INDIA

In the far away state of Meghalaya in the east Khāsi Hills of India, live the Khāsi people who tell this story. Their wealth is passed down from mother to daughter, and many of their gods are female. They worship Ka Sngi, the sun goddess, daughter of their high goddess Mother Nature. The Blue Kingdom of the Sky is a fabulous palace, home of Mother Nature and her four children – Ka Sngi (sun), Ka Ding (fire), U Bnai (moon) and Ka Um (water). Their family life is very human. They feel love and hate, sadness and happiness. In many Indian stories, the Peacock is shown as proud, pompous and fond of luxury. Telling a story about his tail is a sign that there will be a rich marriage in the clan. As for the Old Woman, each Khāsi village has a very wise member who is their leader and fortune teller.

The Blue Peacock lives in the rainforests of India and South East Asia. At breeding time the male displays his spectacular fan tail, which can span 1.5 metres. He feeds on insects, seeds and shoots.

Crane

UGANDA

This story comes from Uganda, in the Lake Region of east Africa. The Sesse Islands are on the west coast of Lake Victoria and there is a town called Namirembe on the southwestern coast of the lake. Uganda was part of a kingdom called Buganda until the 1960s, and royal families like the one in the story were held in high esteem. Kings of Buganda were thought to have superhuman abilities: the King, for example, could give Crane a crest. Myths were told in dance and song by the elders, as the people gathered round a fire. They were told to entertain the listener who could journey far from everyday life into another colourful world, as the Princess does in the story, returning refreshed and happy.

The Crowned Crane is a bird, about 1 metre tall, found in much of Africa on marshes, plains, lakes and seashores. When it breeds, it displays its crest and does a magnificent courtship dance, imitated in the dances of many African peoples. It feeds on fruit, roots, grain and small animals.

How the animals
got their colours
BOLIVIA AND PARAGUAY

This story belongs to the Ayoreo people, who come from the central part of South America which is now Bolivia and Paraguay. Ayoreo stories are thought to be among the most wonderful and dramatic in the world. This story is a part of the Ayoreo 'creation myth', which tells of the beginning of the world and everything in it. In the myth, heaven and earth are created by the sun god. Sun makes the earth by spreading out blankets over the empty universe. When he has finished, he starts to make humans into animals and then gives the animals their colours. Ayoreo myths are sung in praise of a god. This one is in praise of Sun. In other South American mythology, the Jaguar is said to be stupid and slow.

The Jaguar is a spotted big cat, living in South and Central America, usually near water. It is between 1.7 and 2.7 metres long and is a good swimmer, finding its prey in rivers and on land.

The plain brown coloured Puma is slightly smaller than the Jaguar and lives in North and South America in rainforest, forest, prairies and pampas. A fierce night hunter, it feeds on animals as large as deer or elk.

The story does not say what kind of snakes Sun colours. They are most likely to be common South American Rat Snakes. These are about 2.5 metres long and feed on rodents and other small animals.